The Story of Tantrum O'Furrily

Cressida Cowell and Mark Nicholas

Hodder
Children's
Books

For my baby daughter Amelie. Always follow your dreams x -M. N.
To Lily and Baloo -C. C.

HODDER CHILDREN'S BOOKS

First published in Great Britain in 2018 by Hodder and Stoughton

Text © Cressida Cowell, 2018
Illustrations © Mark Nicholas, 2018

The moral rights of the author and illustrator have been asserted.

A CIP catalogue record of this book
is available from the British Library.

ISBN: 978 1 444 93380 2

10 9 8 7 6 5 4 3 2 1

Printed and bound in China.

Hodder Children's Books
An imprint of
Hachette Children's Group
Part of Hodder and Stoughton
Carmelite House
50 Victoria Embankment
London, EC4Y 0DZ

An Hachette UK Company
www.hachette.co.uk

www.hachettechildrens.co.uk

The Story of Tantrum O'Furrily

Cressida Cowell
and
Mark Nicholas

Hodder Children's Books

One wild and windy night a stray cat called Tantrum O'Furrily
and her three hungry kittens were dancing across the rooftops.
"Let me tell you a story," sang Tantrum to the moon.
"Can we EAT a story?" asked the littlest kitten.
"Listen to the story and try to keep up,"
purred Tantrum as she weaved through
the chimney pots.

And THIS was the story
that Tantrum sang:

"Once upon a time there was a kitten called Smallpaw who was very, very lucky.

Smallpaw had a comfy bed and a kind owner and a mouse that squeaked when you pressed it.

Every night after dinner Smallpaw would press her nose
to the window and gaze outside at the darkness.

'Will you tell me a story?' Smallpaw asked her owner
Mrs Worrykin.

'There are no stories in this house,
thank goodness,' she replied.

'Outside live the stray cats. The stray cats are the story cats. The stray cats are BAD cats. They rob food out of dustbins, they steal and beg and fight with dogs.'

Smallpaw tried hard to be a good cat.

But however hard she tried,
Smallpaw was BORED.

One dark night Mrs Worrykin
forgot to shut the catflap.

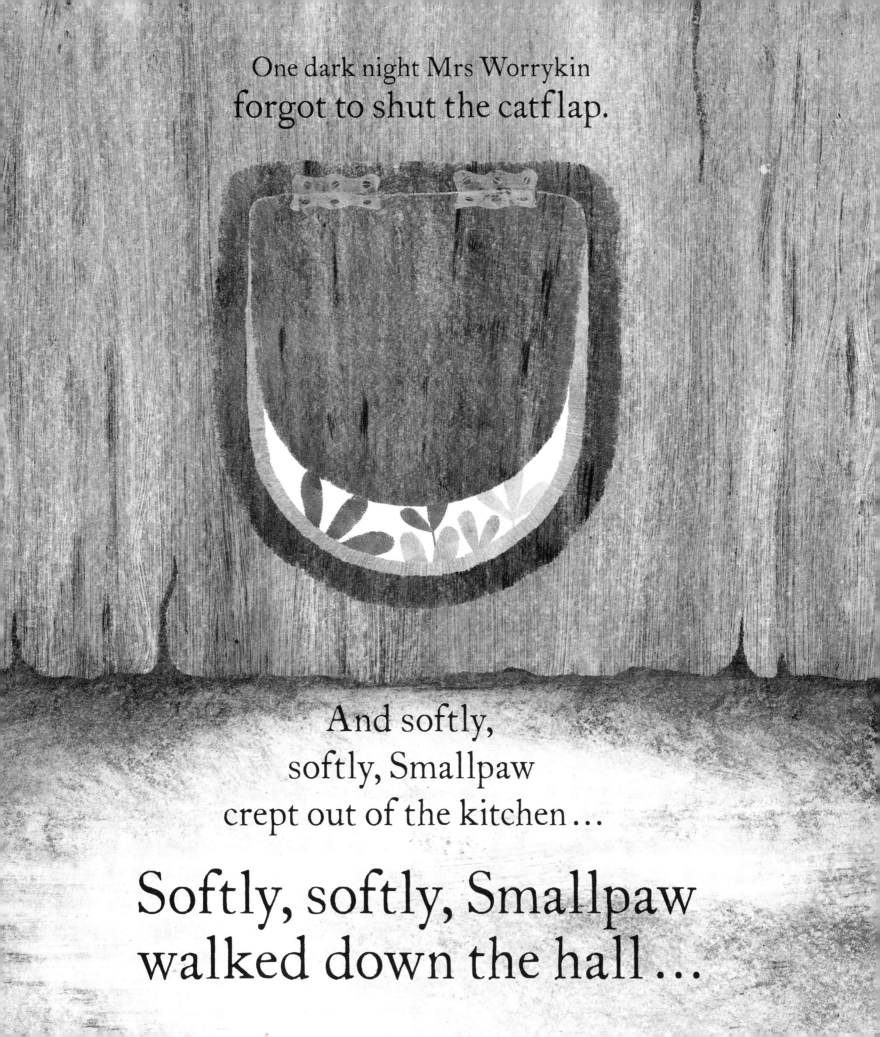

And softly,
softly, Smallpaw
crept out of the kitchen...

Softly, softly, Smallpaw
walked down the hall...

And softly, softly, she put her nose out of the cat flap and into the darkness...

Sniffing, sniffing, sniffing for a story just for her.

And there in the garden lay a fine foxy
animal in a bright red coat.

'Can you tell me a story?' asked Smallpaw.

'Why yes,' smiled the fox. 'I know lots and lots of stories.

Once upon a time there was a delicious little kitten with
fur as soft as butter, who was bored of being indoors,
where there was no moon to sing to ...'

'Ooh!' squealed Smallpaw.
'The kitten in the story is just like me!'

'Is she?' said the fox. 'Fancy that! One night the yummy
little kitten looked out into the garden where she saw
a handsome fox...'

'What happens next?' asked Smallpaw.

'Come a little closer,' said the fox, 'so you can hear me better.'

So brave little Smallpaw crept outside into the darkness.

'Don't be frightened, furry biscuit,'
said the foxy gentleman,
with a smile that showed all of his nice white teeth.
'Stand right next to me, and I can whisper the
ending into your dear little ear.'

So Smallpaw came closer …

and closer …

and closer …

AND …

THEN SUDDENLY …
everything happened very quickly.

'The end of the story is…

I EAT YOU!'

shouted the fox.

He leapt at Smallpaw with a red springing leap.

But before the fox could get to Smallpaw:

'ROOOOOOOOWYOOOWROOWMEOWOOOOOOOMWWW!!!

A stray cat jumped on him in a
flurry of paws and claws and teeth.

The stray cat fought like a tiger,
and the fox ran away.

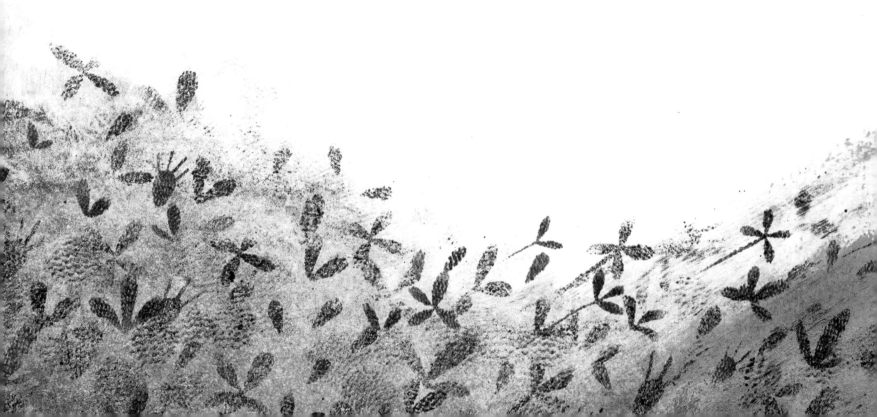

'That doesn't HAVE to be the end of your story,' said the stray cat.
'A cat with courage makes her own story.'

And she disappeared into the night with a swish of her mighty tail.

Well, WHAT a wonderful time Smallpaw had
outside in the garden that night.

And when she came home next morning
Mrs Worrykin was so thankful to see her.

Ever since that night, Mrs Worrykin leaves the catflap open. And happy little Smallpaw goes out every evening, dancing with her new-found friends, singing to the moon.

She is very careful about foxes, and she always comes back.

And Mrs Worrykin puts a saucer of milk by the
cat flap, in case Smallpaw gets hungry …

and Smallpaw always leaves that saucer half-full."

Tantrum O'Furrily stopped at the last chimney pot.
She led her three kittens down the roof of the house...
off the gutter... down the drainpipe...

and they landed in front of a half-full saucer of milk.

"That stray cat was YOU, wasn't it mother?"
"It was indeed. Drink up your milk, kittens.
See how I made the happy ending to our story?
A cat with courage makes her OWN story ...

And be sure to leave a pawprint
on the doorstep to say thank you.
Because you CAN be a stray
cat and a good cat as well."